to the reader

Welcome to the AGS Illustrated Classics!

You are about to enter the world of great literature through pictures as well as words. Now you can actually see the great characters of literature as you read about them!

We want you to know that the costumes, hairstyles, room furnishings, and landscapes have all been carefully researched. No detail has been left out.

As you read, notice that important words are marked with an asterisk (*) and defined at the bottom of the page. Also watch for the scrolls that appear now and then. The scrolls contain important information that will add to your enjoyment of the story.

Now sit back and relax. We know that you will enjoy a great reading experience in the pages that follow.

—The Editors

THE RETURN OF THE NATIVE

Thomas Hardy

AGS®

American Guidance Service, Inc.
Circle Pines, Minnesota 55014-1796
1-800-328-2560

AGS ILLUSTRATED CLASSICS

Collection 1

Black Beauty, The Call of the Wild, Dr. Jekyll and Mr. Hyde, Dracula, Frankenstein, Huckleberry Finn, Moby Dick, The Red Badge of Courage, The Time Machine, Tom Sawyer, Treasure Island, 20,000 Leagues Under the Sea

Collection 2

The Great Adventures of Sherlock Holmes, Gulliver's Travels, The Hunchback of Notre Dame, The Invisible Man, Journey to the Center of the Earth, Kidnapped, The Mysterious Island, The Scarlet Letter, The Story of My Life, A Tale of Two Cities, The Three Musketeers, The War of the Worlds

Collection 3

Around the World in Eighty Days, Captains Courageous, A Connecticut Yankee in King Arthur's Court, The Hound of the Baskervilles, The House of the Seven Gables, Jany Eyre, The Last of the Mohicans, The Best of O. Henry, The Best of Poe, Two Years Before the Mast, White Fang, Wuthering Heights

Collection 4

Ben Hur, A Christmas Carol, The Food of the Gods, Ivanhoe, The Man in the Iron Mask, The Prince and the Pauper, The Prisoner of Zenda, The Return of the Native, Robinson Crusoe, The Scarlet Pimpernel, The Sea Wolf, The Swiss Family Robinson

Collection 5

Billy Budd, Crime and Punishment, Don Quixote, Great Expectations, Heidi, The Iliad, Lord Jim, The Mutiny on Board H.M.S. Bounty, The Odyssey, Oliver Twist, Pride and Prejudice, The Turn of the Screw

Shakespeare Collection

As You Like It, Hamlet, Julius Caesar, King Lear, Macbeth, The Merchant of Venice, A Midsummer Night's Dream, Othello, Romeo and Juliet, The Taming of the Shrew, The Tempest, Twelfth Night

Printed in the United States of America
ISBN 0-7854-0753-7
Product Number 40512
A 0 9 8 7 6 5 4 3 2

about the author

Thomas Hardy, an English novelist and poet, was born in 1840. Until his early thirties, he worked as an architect in London. In the 1870s, however, he left the practice of architecture to devote all his time to writing.

One of his best-known works, *The Return of the Native,* was criticized for its portrayal of human faults. In addition, his idea that men's lives are shaped only by chance happenings drew angry responses from hundreds of readers. *The Return of the Native,* a well-woven tale of love, mishaps and misunderstandings is considered, however, to be his best novel.

Hardy also wrote *Far from the Madding Crowd, The Mayor of Casterbridge* and *Jude the Obscure.* So violent were the attacks against his novels, however, that he turned to writing poetry for the last thirty years of his life. Hardy died in 1928.

Thomas Hardy

THE RETURN OF THE NATIVE

Adapted by
D'ANN CALHOUN FAGO

Illustrated by
FRED CARRILLO

a
VINCENT FAGO
production

Thomasin
Yeobright

Damon
Wildeve

Clym Yeobright

Eustacia
Vye

Mrs. Yeobright

Diggory Venn

It was a gray November afternoon on Egdon Heath in the moor* country of England. The hills had a timeless feeling like the ocean. They seemed to roll on forever.

Through the middle of the heath ran a sandy road that seemed to disappear over a low hill not far away. Along this road walked an old man.

As he walked, he kept watching the road ahead as if seeking a fellow traveler. Finally he caught sight of a cart pulled by two ponies.

The cart was going his way, but was moving so slowly that the old man caught up to it and walked along with its owner. From the red color of the young man, his clothes, and his cart, he knew that his companion was a reddleman.**

*wild, lonely stretches of marsh and grassland also called heaths
**someone who sold red dye to farmers for marking their sheep

The reddleman watched him walk away. Then, looking toward the hills and the sunset, he caught sight of another person. The figure climbed to the top of a hill and stood there.

Suddenly the figure moved away. He could tell that it was a woman.

Soon her reason for leaving became clear. From the other side of the hill, a group of men climbed to the top.

The reddleman saw that they were people from a nearby village. Each carried a large bundle of twigs which they placed together for a bonfire.

And while the men built their fire, a change came over the countryside.

Other bonfires began to glow all over the heath.

Lighting these fires on the fifth of November, just before the cold of winter, was an old custom. * It went back to the earliest people who had lived there, the Druids. **

*a practice handed down from family to family over a long period of time
**a group of priests and wise men who lived in Britain during the first century A.D.

After the first bright blaze of the fire had died down, the people began to talk about local news.

Oh, yes. Thomasin's aunt, Mrs. Yeobright, didn't think Wildeve was good enough!

I hear that the newly-married couple will be back tonight!

You mean Thomasin Yeobright and Damon Wildeve? They had some trouble, didn't they?

That's why they weren't married in the village, wasn't it?

Mrs. Yeobright is too proud! She finally said yes, but she'd already made Wildeve angry.

But her niece Thomasin is a kind and lovely girl.

I hear Mrs. Yeobright's son Clym is coming home for a Christmas visit. He has a fancy job in Paris, I think.

Let's all go down to the inn later and give the new couple a good song!

By this time the bonfire had burned low. Most of those on the other hills were out. Only one bright fire was left.

To be sure, that fire is on the hill by Captain Vye's house.

But he went for a long walk today and must be tired out. I'm sure *he* didn't build it!

Then his granddaughter must have.

She's strange in her ways, living up there by herself. She acts so high and mighty!

Yet she's beautiful— and full of life!

In a few moments some lively dancing began. Sparks flew as couples circled around the dying fire. The only sounds were the cries of the women and the laughter of the men.

Suddenly one of the couples stopped and bid the others be still.

A voice was heard coming from the darkness.

Hal-oo-oo!

Then, in the light of the coals, the dancers saw the reddleman step forth. He was red from head to toe and looked much like the devil himself.

Is there a path through here to Mrs. Yeobright's house?

Yes. It is rough, but if you're careful you can make it.

The reddleman thanked them and left. He had been gone only a few minutes when Mrs. Yeobright came up.

Why, Mrs. Yeobright! A reddleman was just here asking the way to your house.

I may miss him, then, because I'm going toward my niece's new home. If Olly Dowden's here, she might want to walk part way with me.

I'm here, Mrs. Yeobright. I'd be happy to go with you.

They walked together until they reached a place where the road branched.* Mrs. Yeobright followed the straight track which led to the Quiet Woman Inn.

*split in two

As Mrs. Yeobright reached the inn, she saw the reddleman and his cart coming toward her.

You must be looking for me. I am Mrs. Yeobright.

I am Diggory Venn, the reddleman. I am a friend of your niece, Thomasin.

Thomasin has just come back here with her new husband.

No, ma'am. She's here, in the back of my cart! I met her in Anglebury this morning.

She was crying and asked me to bring her home. I think she finally fell asleep.

Let me see her at once!

When she looked into the cart, Mrs. Yeobright saw the young girl, covered with a cloak and sound asleep. But moments later Thomasin awoke and saw her aunt.

The young girl climbed from the cart. After thanking Venn for his help, Mrs. Yeobright spoke sternly to her niece.

I ran away because I was upset. Then I saw Diggory Venn and asked him for a ride.

Let us go inside and talk with Damon.

Thomasin! What is the meaning of this? Why aren't you with Damon?

Our marriage license* was made out wrong. We didn't know it until it was too late.

They found him in the parlor.

What do you mean to do about me?

My dearest Tamsie, I mean to marry you as soon as I can!

Just then they heard the group from the bonfire coming to sing to the young couple. Wildeve went out to the public room to greet them.

When he returned to the parlor, Thomasin and her aunt had gone.

*a paper which gives a couple the right to be married

Meanwhile, since the villagers had left the hill, the woman seen there earlier returned. She stood as if waiting for something—or someone.

At last she went back to the bonfire that the heath people had said was Captain Vye's. Feeding the fire with wood was a small boy, Johnny Nunsuch.

I'm glad you're back, Miss Eustacia.

I'll send you home soon. Has anybody been here?

Your grandfather, Captain Vye, came looking for you.

But this was not the answer Eustacia wanted. Soon, however, came the signal she was waiting for, and she sent Johnny home. The man who came toward her was Damon Wildeve.

I saw your bon-fire and knew it was meant for me.

Eustacia Vye was pleased that the fire had drawn this man to her, but she tried not to show it.

How did you know it was for you? I've had no word since you said you were going to marry Thomasin Yeobright.

I had given you up until I heard the news! I knew you couldn't marry her and had to come back to me.

How did you hear this? Does anyone else know?

My grandfather guessed it from something that happened today on one of his long walks.

Damon, tell me that you didn't marry Thomasin because you love me best!

I haven't married her yet, and I came to your call! If you wish it, I will take you from this place that you hate.

Eustacia promised to give him her answer in two weeks. Then they parted.

Meanwhile, Johnny Nunsuch was on his way home. But he was frightened by a strange light in one of the hollows and ran back to Eustacia.

Before reaching the bonfire, he stopped and saw that Eustacia had a visitor, a man. He waited for a few minutes and then walked quietly away.

This time, as he tried to circle around the light, he stumbled and fell. He landed at the feet of the reddleman who was sitting on the steps of his cart.

Who are you?

I am Johnny Nunsuch, sir!

The reddleman helped Johnny up. To calm the boy, he told him about his work, selling red dye to sheep farmers. Then Johnny told him about seeing Eustacia and the man.

What were they talking about?

The man told Miss Eustacia he liked her best and would take her away from here.

When Johnny was safely on his way home, the reddleman sat thinking for a long time.

Then he took out an old letter from Thomasin. Two years ago he had asked her to marry him. In her letter she had refused.

So Diggory had taken up the lonely life of a reddleman. But he still loved Thomasin and could not bear to see her unhappy.

I am very sorry your friend Tamsin.

The letter looked worn, as though it had been read many times.

The next morning Diggory Venn went calling on Eustacia Vye. He begged her to give up Damon Wildeve.

He would marry Thomasin at once if it were not for you!

I will never give him up, never!

So Diggory made a different plan. He went to see Mrs. Yeobright.

I would like to marry Thomasin. I have loved her for two years.

If Thomasin doesn't marry Wildeve, it will hurt her good name. Besides, she is in love with the man.

But the reddleman's offer pleased Mrs. Yeobright. She immediately went to speak with Damon Wildeve.

Mrs. Yeobright could tell that Wildeve was upset by this news. The idea of losing Thomasin to someone else made him want to keep her.

Another man has asked to marry Thomasin. I want to be sure you will not stand in the way.

I'll give her up if you wish. But I thought I was to be her husband.

I do not want you to see Thomasin again until you are sure of your plans.

I need one more day, and then I will let you know.

In the evening Wildeve met Eustacia at their old spot.

I must know if you are leaving this place with me!

Why? You gave me two weeks to make up my mind.

Another man wants to marry Thomasin, and I must know my plans.

And you come for me because you are not sure of her? You will have to wait for my answer.

Later, when Captain Vye came back from the village, he had news for his granddaughter.

Where has he been all these years?

Young Clym Yeobright is coming to spend Christmas with his mother.

In Paris. He is a manager for a diamond merchant.

Since the next afternoon was clear, three of the heath men were stacking hardwood and furze* outside of Captain Vye's house.

The men talked as they worked. Everything they said came to Eustacia's ears down the chimney.

Clym Yeobright is a clever man. He has more book learning than anyone else around here!

Except Miss Eustacia. She knows as much as anybody else.

They'd make a good pair, wouldn't they? Clym's family is as good as hers is!

Eustacia gave much thought to the stranger the men had spoken of. Finally she walked to a hill near the Yeobright house and stood there until evening.

What will this man from Paris think about the heath now? Will he take me out of here?

*the wood of the evergreen shrubs that grow on moors

At the Yeobright house, where the man from Paris was expected, Thomasin climbed to the loft where they stored apples for the winter.

I'll bring down some russets,* Aunt. Clym always loved them.

As soon as you're finished, we'll go for the holly.

Thomasin and her aunt walked to where the holly grew. Soon the girl had cut a good number of full branches.

Will you walk with me to meet Clym this evening?

I would like that. But Aunt, you must promise not to tell him about my marriage to Damon. I want to tell him myself.

Later, the two women set out again. They walked along the way on which Clym was to return.

*a kind of apple

Meanwhile, as evening came, Eustacia headed home. In the dark she heard voices nearby.

It was Mrs. Yeobright and Thomasin. But a man's voice greeted her.

Good evening!

Eustacia tried to see him clearly, but had no light, and the group went on. Yet meeting the stranger even in such a way was exciting.

At home later, Eustacia questioned her grandfather.

Why aren't we friendly with the Yeobrights?

I think you would find them too much like the other farm people nearby.

I thought Mrs. Yeobright was a lady, not like most of the women on the heath.

Yes, but her husband was a rough sort of man. She became used to living the way her husband did.

That night Eustacia dreamed of the young man from Paris. He was a knight in silver armor and he had danced with her.

I wish that I had seen his face!

Several days passed, and Eustacia had not yet seen Clym Yeobright. She knew that he would soon be leaving, and thus was about to give up. Then something happened that gave her an idea. She was at home alone when Charley, a young heath boy, came to the door.

Who is it?

It's me, Charley. I have a favor to ask!

Charley often worked for Captain Vye. He told Eustacia that he had been given a part in the Christmas play. One of the performances would be at the Yeobrights' Christmas party.

Last year your grandfather let us practice in the barn.

I know. You may use it now if you like.

As Eustacia thought about the play, given every year at Christmas time, she made a plan.

Charley, would you let me take your part on the night of the Christmas party?

But Miss Eustacia—you couldn't!

I could if I wore your costume. All of the players wear masks over their faces!

Well, all right, Miss Eustacia. I will do the best I can.

Eustacia was happy. This would be an adventure, and at the same time she would see Clym Yeobright.

On the night of the Christmas party, the players waited in the Vye's barn dressed as crusaders. * All had arrived but Charley, the Turkish knight. ** This evening, however, he and Eustacia had planned for her to come in late.

Twenty minutes past eight and Charley's not here!

He'll come, though. Don't worry!

A moment later Eustacia appeared at the door dressed in Charley's costume. The players blew out their candles and set out for the Yeobrights' house.

The moon threw a bright light upon the strange figures walking on the moor.

The players entered the house and found that the guests had all moved to one end of the room. A large place was left for a stage.

When it was time for her part, Eustacia held her head high. She spoke her lines in as deep a voice as she could. When she had finished, she stood back looking for Clym.

*knights who fought to free the Holy Land from the Arabs during the Middle Ages
**a soldier from Turkey, a country on the Mediterranean Sea

And finally Eustacia found him, leaning against a bench. She knew right away that this was Clym Yeobright.

When the play was over, Mrs. Yeobright invited the actors to sit down for supper before they left.

It's a cold night. My son and I would like to serve you something warm.

Surely you will have some!

No, thank you.

Forgive him. He's only a boy.

Eustacia slipped out the door to wait for the others. But Clym followed her.

Are you a woman, or am I wrong?

Yes, I am a woman.

Just then the other players came out and Clym wished them all a good night.

The next day Eustacia met the reddleman as she walked on the heath. Wildeve had told her about Venn's offer to marry Thomasin.

Good morning, reddleman! Are you staying here because you hope to marry Thomasin Yeobright?

I love her, it's true. But if she is not happy without Wildeve, I will do my best to help her marry *him.*

We agree at last! I, too, would like to see them wed.

And so it came about that Diggory Venn brought a note from Eustacia to Damon Wildeve. Wildeve was shocked at what he read.

I dont want to see you again

Eustacia

Later, Venn went to the Yeobright house. But Wildeve had arrived first.

I'm going to set the wedding date with Thomasin right now!

The reddleman was not surprised that Wildeve had refused to lose both women.

That same evening, Thomasin and her aunt were talking. Clym Yeobright was away visiting a friend at the time.

When Wildeve knocked at the door, Thomasin went out and spoke with him. Then she returned to her aunt.

Damon wants us to be married at once. And I agreed.

Yes, I thought that might be Damon at the door.

Clym had written his mother saying he had heard stories about Thomasin being jilted* on her wedding day. He was angry. Both Thomasin and her aunt felt bad about this.

Then the wedding will be on the morning Clym comes home.

Yes, it will be over before he even gets here.

Clym returned home a few days later to find that Thomasin was at the church being married. He scolded his mother for not having told him about it sooner. Then Diggory Venn arrived.

Thomasin is now Mrs. Damon Wildeve. I was there to see them married.

I hope she will be happy!

*left at the altar without the groom

On the following Sunday some of the heath men were having their hair cut. It was a great time for neighborhood gossip.* Clym had been out walking, but seeing the men together, he went over and joined them.

Now folks, let me guess who you've been talking about!

We were talking about you. What's keeping you here on the heath?

Yes, this is no place for a diamond shop.

I'll tell you. I've come back to stay because I think I can be useful here. I'm tired of selling jewels to rich people.

I've come back to start a school and help the people I know best.

And Clym started again on his walk across the heath. He had given the men something to talk about.

He'll never be able to do it!

What will Mrs. Yeobright say?

It's good-hearted of the young man. But I think he should stay with the diamond business.

*talk about local news

When Clym had reached home again, he found his mother inside.

I've something to tell you, Mother. I'm not going back to Paris. I've given up my work there.

Why didn't you tell me sooner?

Because I was not sure of myself yet. But as a teacher to the poor heath people I would be happy.

This doesn't please me, Clym. You could have become a rich man.

As Clym and his mother talked, one of the heath men came to the door. He had news about something that had happened that morning at church.

Susan Nunsuch stuck a needle into the arm of Miss Eustacia Vye. She said Miss Vye had bewitched* her children.

How terrible!

Mother, don't you see they need a teacher?

Not long after, Sam the turfcutter** stopped by.

Captain Vye's bucket has dropped into the well. We have some rope but need more. They've had enough trouble already today.

Our rope is in the shed. Take what you need.

I'll help.

As the two men got the rope, Sam talked about Eustacia Vye.

You ought to see Miss Vye. Such a beauty!

I will join you later.

*cast a spell upon
**a person who cuts blocks of turf or peat from the ground to use as fuel

Later Clym walked over to Captain Vye's house to help. When the men were finished, Eustacia came out to thank them. The others left, but Clym stayed behind to talk with her.

I think we've met before. I heard what happened to you today and I am sorry.

This was the first of many meetings between Clym and Eustacia. They walked every day upon the heath and soon fell in love.

But Clym's mother was not happy. She knew that Eustacia Vye had something to do with Clym's staying on the heath.

For days we have spoken hardly a word. Why, mother?

When I see how wrong you are about this girl, I think you are wrong about other things.

Mother, we are in love and plan to marry. Let's say no more.

You are blinded by that woman, Clym!

During the day Clym worked at his desk. But he met Eustacia every evening.

My Eustacia!

Clym, dearest!

They spoke of their love for each other.

I love you, Clym! But your mother is not happy that I do.

That does not matter. You must be my wife!

And whenever they talked about marrying, Eustacia asked Clym about Paris.

Tell me about the Louvre.*

Clym walked home later filled with love, but also with fear. He wasn't sure that his plans to live a simple life on the heath would make Eustacia happy.

*a famous museum in Paris

Clym was studying one spring day when his mother came to him.

Thomasin says that you and Eustacia Vye are planning to marry soon.

We're planning on being married, but it may not be soon.

Will you take her to Paris?

No. We will live here and I will teach school.

Then, Clym, I wish you would leave my house and go to the only person you seem to love!

I do not want to leave you. But I don't want to make you unhappy.

Later Clym went to meet Eustacia. He had hoped to have his mother with him.

Eustacia, let us be married at once. First we will live in a tiny cottage, but things will be better later.

Now Clym had a woman to fight for. But he was also sad about his mother.

The next morning Clym went across the heath and found a little house to rent. Then he went to say goodbye to his mother.

Mother, I am leaving. Eustacia and I will be married. I want you to come and see us.

I do not think I shall come.

Then it will not be my fault. Goodbye!

After Clym left, his mother cried. Later, when Thomasin came to see her, Mrs. Yeobright spoke of the money which would one day belong to Thomasin and Clym. Then she spoke of her son.

Thomasin, do you think he hates me?

Of course not! It is only that he loves Eustacia so much!

About the same time, Damon Wildeve talked with the driver of a cart that had pulled up before the inn. The driver had news.

Miss Eustacia Vye and Mr. Yeobright are getting married right away.

Wildeve was surprised and a little sad at losing Eustacia.

Clym's mother did not go to the wedding. But when it was over, Damon Wildeve stopped by and asked for the money she had promised Thomasin.

It isn't ready yet.

I don't think you trust me!

The young husband lured* Christian into a game of dice. Soon Christian had lost all of the money.

Later Mrs. Yeobright gave the money to Christian Cantle. Half was to go to Clym and half to Thomasin at the wedding party. On the way, Christian met Wildeve.

Christian ran away. But as Wildeve gathered the money together, the reddleman came forward.

*tempted

Venn sat down where Christian had been. Without a word he took a coin from his pocket and laid it on the stone.

You heard our game?

Put your money down and let's play— if you dare!

I've doubled your bet!

With money that's not your own!

Wildeve grew nervous, but Venn was as calm as a stone. The reddleman kept winning.

Venn finally won all the money back. Then he gathered it up and left.

Later, as Thomasin returned from the wedding party, he gave her the money. Neither knew that half of it should have gone to Clym.

The weeks flew by and it was summer. Clym and Eustacia were happy and Clym studied hard.

Thomasin wrote to her aunt, thanking her for the money. But Mrs. Yeobright didn't hear from Clym. Afraid that Eustacia might have taken Clym's money, Mrs. Yeobright went to see her. They met on the path.

I was coming to see you.

I am here on business only. Did Thomasin's husband give you some money?

Money from Mr. Wildeve? No! Never!

Don't get angry at me, young woman! I'm a poor mother who has lost a son.

You need not have lost him at all.

There was nothing left to say. Mrs. Yeobright left, and Eustacia stood alone on the moor.

Then Eustacia ran home to Clym. He could tell she was upset.

I have seen your mother, and I won't see her again. She asked if I had taken money from Damon Wildeve!

There must be a mistake!

Oh, Clym! I hate this place! Take me to Paris!

We can't leave, Eustacia. I'm staying here to teach!

But as summer wore on, Clym's eyes grew sore from studying so hard. To make a little money, he began cutting roots for firewood.

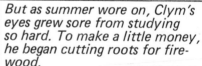

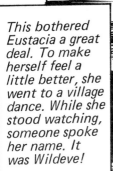

Will you dance with me?

This bothered Eustacia a great deal. To make herself feel a little better, she went to a village dance. While she stood watching, someone spoke her name. It was Wildeve!

It was magic to both of them. When it was time for her to start home, Wildeve walked along with her.

Not far away they saw Clym and Diggory walking toward them. Wildeve told Eustacia good night and moved quickly away.

Meanwhile, Diggory was sure he had seen Wildeve with Eustacia. To check this, he went to the inn and found only Thomasin at home.

Thomasin told the reddleman that her husband was away. Now Venn knew that Wildeve had been with Eustacia.

Later he went to tell Mrs. Yeobright about Clym's bad sight. He begged her to visit Clym and Eustacia for the good of all.

He is my only son! I will go.

Believe me, ma'am, you will be glad you did.

At this very time Clym and Eustacia were talking about the same thing.

I must make up with my mother. She is getting old and she is alone.

What will you do?

I will go to see her tomorrow!

The next morning Mrs. Yeobright started the long walk to her son's house. It was a hot day.

After walking a long time, she saw a man ahead of her. It was her son! She saw him reach his house and go in.

His walk is like my husband's used to be.

By this time she was weak from the heat. She sat down on a little hill above the house to rest a bit. Then she saw another man go into the house. After a few minutes, Mrs. Yeobright started down.

Meanwhile, Wildeve, who was the second man Mrs. Yeobright had seen enter her son's house, was talking to Eustacia.

Is Clym at home?

Yes, but he's asleep. He begins working early in the morning and then comes home to sleep. Come in.

It was clear that he wanted to speak to her in private.

The young man told Eustacia that he still loved her. But just then there was a knock at the door, and Eustacia looked out the window.

It's Mrs. Yeobright! What shall I do?

Let me out through the back door! Surely Clym will wake up and let her in!

Quickly Eustacia led Wildeve out the back way. When she finally opened the front door, Mrs. Yeobright had gone.

Clym's mother started back home, but she could hardly walk. After a while she met a little boy who felt sorry for her but didn't know what to do.

You don't look very well! Is something the matter?

I am a broken-hearted woman cast off* by my son!

Johnny Nunsuch walked on. Soon she grew so tired that she collapsed.**

*left alone, thrown away
**fainted, could not get up again

After Mrs. Yeobright had left, Eustacia went into the room where Clym slept. She sat there quietly until he awoke.

I dreamed that my mother was calling for help. I am going to her house this evening.

Later, Clym started out. About halfway across the heath he heard someone moaning. Drawing near, he found his mother lying on the ground.

Mother, how did you get here? Don't you know me?

Clym went for help to some nearby cottages. One of the men ran for the doctor.

It's not only her heart! She's been bitten by a snake!

It will take too long for the doctor! We'll have to use our own ways.

The heath people did what they could. For snake bite they always used hot fat from another snake. Susan Nunsuch ran for her frying pan.

While Eustacia waited for Clym, her grandfather drove up with some news.

Have you heard about Mr. Wildeve's fortune?*

His uncle in Canada died and left him a lot of money!

When her grandfather left, Eustacia grew tired of waiting for Clym and started across the heath. On the way she met Wildeve.

I'm happy to hear of your good fortune. What will you do now?

I will travel—first to Paris, then to Italy, then . . . who knows?

As they walked, they came to a group of people. Standing back in the shadows, they listened to find out what was happening. Eustacia saw Clym. Then a child's voice cried out.

I spoke to that lady today. She said her son didn't love her any more!

Just then some women started to cry and the doctor announced that Mrs. Yeobright was dead.

*riches

For three weeks after his mother's funeral,* Clym was very sick.

I never went to her house, so she never came to mine. She never knew how welcome she would have been!

One day Thomasin came to visit him. She told Clym and Eustacia that her baby would be born in a month. But all Clym talked about was his dead mother.

I did nothing to help her. I don't deserve to live, and Eustacia would be better off if I died!

Let me talk. Maybe I can comfort you before my husband comes for me.

At the sound of wheels on the driveway below, Eustacia ran down to tell Wildeve that his wife would soon be there. But her real wish was to speak to him alone.

I can't talk to anyone but you. Nobody else knows of my real trouble!

Poor girl! When he is better, tell him what you know. But don't tell him I was there when his mother came.

*a church service for someone who has died

Slowly Clym began to feel better. He was in his garden when one of the heath men came to tell him about Thomasin's baby girl. He also told Clym that Diggory Venn had talked with his mother the day before she died.

Then I must see Venn to find out where she was going!

But he's been away since then.

The next day Clym visited his mother's house into which he and Eustacia were planning to move. When Diggory Venn suddenly appeared, they were both surprised.

I knew nothing of your mother's death. But I am sure she was on her way to visit you!

The next day Clym paid a visit to little Johnny Nunsuch, the boy who said he had seen Mrs. Yeobright on the heath the day she died. Johnny's mother called the boy in.

Where did you first see the woman?

At your house!

What did she do?

What do you think of your wife now?

She saw a gentleman go into the house a while after you did. Then she went and knocked at the door. A lady with black hair looked out the window, but nobody opened the door. So she left.

Clym ran back over the heath to Eustacia. As he came up behind her, she saw his face in the mirror—wild and angry.

You know! I see it in your face.

Who was the man with you when you shut the door against my mother?

Eustacia grew pale at his look.

I'll never tell you, though I could clear myself by speaking. I will leave this house instead.

Eustacia had not been gone long when a maid came from Thomasin Wildeve with news.

Mrs. Wildeve and her new baby are getting along well. The baby is to be named Eustacia.

Meanwhile, Eustacia had no idea where to go or what to do. She went to her grandfather's house, but it was closed and locked. Charley was working around the stable.

You don't look well, ma'am! Can I help?

I would like to get into the house.

Charley squeezed in through a window. In about an hour Eustacia lay on a couch in front of the fire, and Charley brought her something to eat.

You are very kind, Charley.

Well, you've been kind to me.

A little later Eustacia saw some loaded guns hanging in Captain Vye's room. Charley saw her looking at them for a long time. Later . . .

Where are the guns that were hanging in this corner?

I locked them up. You seemed too broken-hearted this morning, and I care too much for you to let you have them.

I will not use them, I promise. Please don't tell anyone!

And Charlie gave Eustacia his word.

Charley did everything he could to keep Eustacia happy. He felt he had to take care of her.

From the heath he brought arrowheads, moss, * and crystals** for her to see. A week passed.

Eustacia hardly ever went out of the house. She did not notice what was going on around her.

One evening her grandfather came back from the village and told her that Clym Yeobright had moved to his mother's old house.

Eustacia felt more cut off from life than ever.

On the evening of November fifth, the night the heath people always built their bonfires, Charley built one for Eustacia. He knew she had enjoyed this before.

But Charley didn't know that Eustacia's bonfires had been a signal to Wildeve.

*small wild plants
**shiny stones that look like diamonds

When Eustacia came out she told Charley to let the fire die. But as Eustacia stood watching the coals, Wildeve appeared.

I didn't light this fire! Don't come to me here!

I can't bear to see you so unhappy. How can I help?

I must get away from this place!

I am willing to be your friend and help you— or to go away with you forever! You must choose.

You can help me as a friend. When I signal some evening at eight o'clock, it will mean that at midnight I want to leave this place. Please bring your horse and carriage.

I will be watching every night at eight.

Then Wildeve went back to his home.

Meanwhile Clym began to wish Eustacia would return to him. On the evening of November fifth he went to see Thomasin and her husband to ask their advice. Only Thomasin was there.

Have you heard that Eustacia has left me?

Perhaps you were too hard on her. Ask her to come back!

When Clym returned home he wrote a letter to Eustacia. He told her that he loved her still and wanted her to return.

There! If she doesn't come on her own by tomorrow night, I will send it.

When Wildeve reached his house, Thomasin told him she had heard a rumor* that he was seeing Eustacia again. Wildeve grew angry and Thomasin began to cry.

Let's not speak of this any more!

*a piece of news that has not been proved, but is supposed to be kept secret

The next evening, Eustacia decided to leave Egdon Heath. She thought Clym would never forgive her.

She sent a signal to Wildeve, then waited quietly in her room until midnight. By then a bad storm had started.

Captain Vye thought Eustacia was asleep and put the letter where she would find it in the morning.

I won't bother her now.

While Eustacia was resting, someone stopped by with Clym's letter.

At midnight, Eustacia started out into the storm to meet Wildeve. She had no money and no plans, and she didn't really want to go away with Wildeve.

The storm raging outside was like the storm she felt deep within her.

On that same evening Susan Nunsuch was sitting up late. Her child Johnny was sick.

Susan had seen Eustacia pass her door earlier, and soon afterward her son had called out in pain.

Mother, I feel so bad! Can you do something?

Susan knew exactly what to do. She was sure Eustacia was a witch, and she had an old remedy* to use against her. Carefully, Susan made a woman's figure out of soft wax. Then she asked Johnny a question.

In her sewing basket Susan found some red ribbon which she tied around the figure's neck. Then she stuck pins into the doll.

Did you notice, dear, what Miss Eustacia wore the last time you saw her?

I know she wore a red ribbon around her neck.

There, my high and mighty lady! You and your spells** have been broken!

With the fire tongs Susan held the figure over the flames until it melted away. As she did this, she repeated the Lord's Prayer backwards three times. Her work was now done.

*something to cure a sick person
**magic powers

Meanwhile, Clym Yeobright waited.

Though the night was wild with rain and wind, he hoped Eustacia might come in answer to his letter.

Then there was a knock on the door. It was Thomasin carrying her baby wrapped well against the storm.

Thomasin!

I am afraid that my husband is going away with Eustacia! I need your help!

Thomasin told Clym that Wildeve had left on a trip that night.

He had told her he would return the next day, but he had taken a great deal of money with him.

Please Clym, go talk with him! He is at the stable getting the carriage ready.

Stay here and dry yourself. I'll go at once.

*Just then Captain Vye arrived, worried about Eustacia. Charley had told him about her thoughts of suicide. **

Where are your guns now?

Safely locked up. But there are other ways.

So the two men set out to look for Eustacia and Wildeve.

*killing oneself

But Thomasin couldn't stay still. She wrapped the baby and started for home.

Why, it's Diggory Venn's van surely!

On the path ahead of her, in a small hollow, she saw a light.

I heard you go past before. Why were you crying so?

Oh, Diggory, don't you know me? It's Thomasin—and I haven't been near here before!

I lost my way coming from Clym's house. Can you show me my path home?

Of course! I will go with you. Let me carry the baby.

As they walked along, Diggory told her that he had heard a woman passing by only a few moments before.

She had been weeping. He had tried to find her.

There is the inn light. You can go back now.

No, that light is south of the inn, and the millpond* lies between us. You could easily walk into it. I will take you.

*a small lake fed by a swift-flowing stream

Earlier, on the other side of the heath, Wildeve had seen Eustacia's signal and had prepared for the trip. Shortly before midnight he waited near the millpond for Eustacia.

The water was roaring, but Wildeve heard footsteps nearby. It was Clym. Just then the two men heard a sound like something falling into the water.

Can it be Eustacia?

The men raced to the millpond. Wildeve, who saw something in the rough waters, jumped in and disappeared. Clym tried a quieter spot, but he, too, was pulled under.

The three bodies were carried to the inn. The doctor did what he could for them.

At this moment Diggory and Thomasin arrived. Diggory jumped into the pond and pulled both men from the water. Later they found the body of Eustacia.

Only Clym is still alive!

Later, Diggory Venn sat by the fire at the inn. He watched a servant woman hanging rows of small, wet papers before the fire to dry.

What are they?

The poor master's money. This was all in his pockets.

Early in the morning there was a gentle knock at the door. Charley came to ask if anything had been heard of Eustacia. Venn told him the sad news.

May I see her once more?

Yes, you may. You too, Diggory. Follow me.

I spoke harshly to her, and she left. I should have drowned too!

No, Clym. You have always meant well!

Now Clym was left alone in the world. During the following months he thought often about the rest of his life.

58

Meanwhile, the story of Wildeve and Eustacia became a legend. * Thomasin and her child lived in Mrs. Yeobright's house with Clym.

One day Diggory Venn came to call. A year had passed since Thomasin or Clym had seen him. In that time he had bought a farm and was no longer a reddleman. Diggory asked if the village maypole ** could be set up in a field nearby.

On the day of the maypole dancing, Thomasin watched from the house. She saw Diggory Venn taking part in most of the dances.

Diggory was the last person to leave. Clym invited him into the house.

Thank you, but I must find a glove dropped by one of the young ladies.

Later, from her room, Thomasin saw Venn pick up a glove and put it into his pocket.

I am surprised that he should worry about a silly glove!

*a story passed along by word of mouth
**a tall, narrow pole around which people danced on May 1 to celebrate spring

Thomasin seemed very quiet during the next few days. Once Clym asked her what the trouble was.

Are you worried about something?

Oh no. I just wonder who Diggory Venn is so much in love with.

That afternoon Thomasin was going for a walk. When she could not find one of her new gloves, she called for the young girl who looked after her child.

Rachel, have you seen my new gloves?

Oh, ma'am—I used them on maypole day and lost one. I will buy you a new pair.

I told Mr. Venn they were yours. He gave me money for a new pair. I will get them, ma'am!

Thomasin was pleased to learn that the glove Diggory had been so careful to find was her own. The next day, when she and her little girl were having a picnic, Diggory rode up.

Diggory, give me my glove!

Diggory gave Thomasin her glove. They talked, and he told her he was still in love with her.

I would like to marry you if you will have me.

Later . . .

Clym, I am thinking of marrying Diggory Venn.

If you love him, then go ahead.

So Thomasin and Diggory's wedding day was set. At Timothy Fairway's house, the men gathered to make a present for the couple, a feather bed.*

It's going to be a good bed by the look of it!

So 'tis, so 'tis. We're putting in seventy pounds of the best feathers.

*a mattress stuffed with goose, duck, and chicken feathers

Clym was the minister at the wedding. The wedding party, held at his house, was lively with dancing, singing, food, and drink. Before the bride and groom drove off to their new home, Thomasin spoke softly to Clym.

Now we leave you in your own house again! But we are never far from you.

Thomasin and Diggory had a happy life together.

The Sunday after the wedding, something new was seen on the heath. On one of the highest hills a man stood preaching.

Clym had finally found his new way of life.

words to know

crystals	bewitched	remedy
cast off	Druids	suicide
lured	rumor	legend

questions

1. When Clym Yeobright, the "native," returned to his home on Egdon Heath, what were his plans for the future?

2. What did Eustacia Vye want most of all?

3. The heath people held many strange beliefs and followed customs their families had practiced for hundreds of years. Name three of these beliefs or customs.

4. In what way were the Vyes and Yeobrights different from most of the heath people?

5. Who did Damon Wildeve really love—Thomasin or Eustacia—or both? What kind of a man was he?

6. Thomas Hardy, who wrote *The Return of the Native*, believed that most things happen in people's lives only by chance or luck. Name at least three chance happenings in the story and tell how each one affected the characters' lives.

7. Clym Yeobright was the only character in the story who had a real plan for his life. Did his plan work out? What happened to him at the end of the story?

8. Diggory Venn is a good example of a person who lets life happen to him and does little to change things one way or another. What happened to him at the end of the story? Did his life bear out what Thomas Hardy says about chance or luck?